Science Close-Up

MAGNETS

By Robert Bell
Illustrated by Barbara Steadman

A GOLDEN BOOK • NEW YORK
Western Publishing Company, Inc., Racine, Wisconsin 53404

© 1995 Western Publishing Company, Inc. Illustrations © 1995 Barbara Steadman. All rights reserved.
Printed in the U.S.A. No part of this book may be reproduced or copied in any form without written
permission from the publisher. All trademarks are the property of Western Publishing Company, Inc.
Library of Congress Catalog Card Number: 94-73825 ISBN: 0-307-12862-8   A MCMXCV

Long ago in China, someone found a rock with a sense of direction.

The discoverer—nobody knows who it was—put a sliver of this rock on top of a piece of wood or cork and floated it in water. The wood slowly turned—by itself! It turned one way, then the other. Finally it stopped, as though the sliver of rock needed to point in only one direction.

It was the first compass. The needle of a compass always points north, no matter which way the compass is turned.

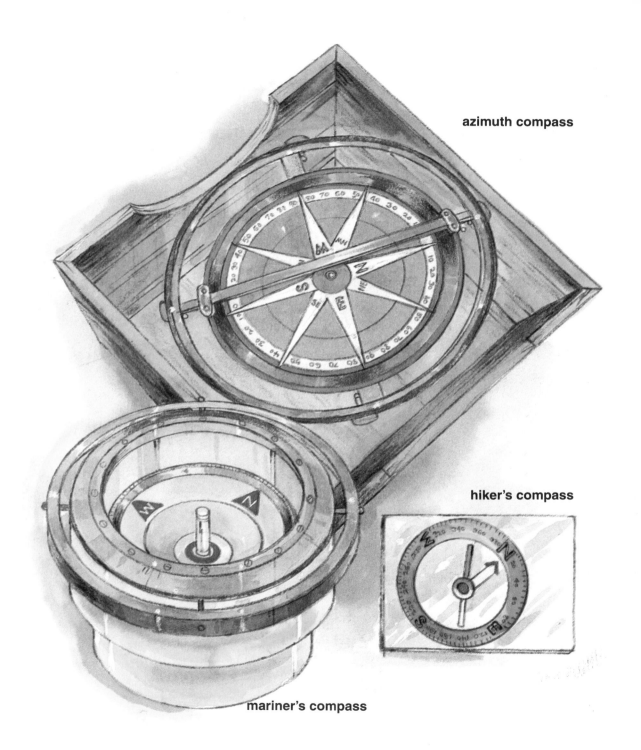

azimuth compass

hiker's compass

mariner's compass

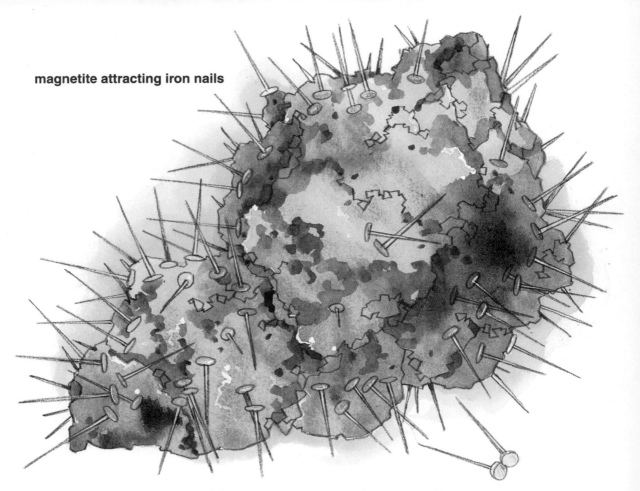

magnetite attracting iron nails

What Is a Magnet?

That unknown Chinese inventor was not using just any rock. The mysterious dark-colored rock had the power to make other objects move without touching them! The rock was a kind of natural magnet called **magnetite**.

Magnets can do two things. They can *attract* other things or pull them closer. Magnets can also *repel* things or push them away.

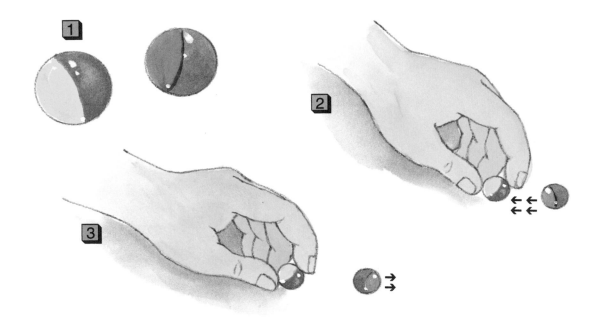

Try It Yourself!

Push Me, Pull You

Use the magnetic marbles that came with this book to see what magnets can do:

1. Place two marbles on a table, several inches apart.
2. Pick up one marble and hold it between your thumb and forefinger so that the green side faces out. Bring that marble close to the other marble. Which color does it attract?
Turn around the marble you are holding so that the yellow side faces out. Which color does it attract?
3. Which colors repel each other?

Invisible Force

How did the marble in your hand push or pull the other marbles without touching them?

There must be something—a **force**—that reaches from one magnet to another. You can't see, hear, smell, taste, or touch this force. But you know it's there, because you feel it pull the magnets toward each other.

This force is called **magnetism**. And if you could see it, it would look like this.

It is possible to demonstrate the pull of the magnetic force. To do so, arrange four pencils in a square with the points touching the erasers. Place a bar magnet in the middle of the square. Then lay a sheet of white paper over the pencils and the magnet.

Wearing rubber gloves, gently rub two pieces of steel wool together, about 6 inches above the paper, so that the steel wool dust falls onto the paper.

The steel dust shows the curved lines of the force that surround the magnet.

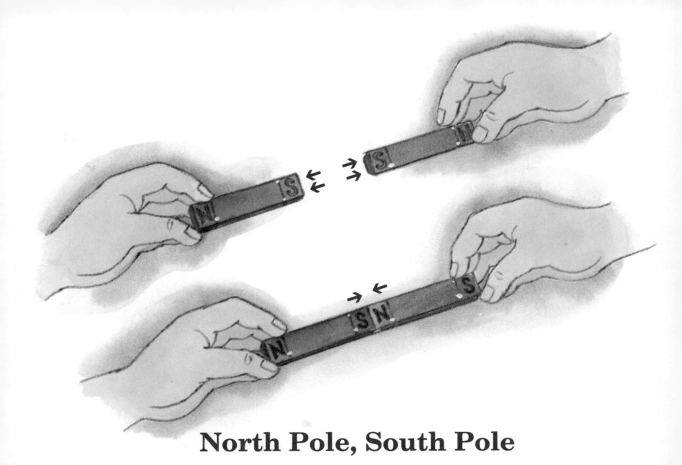

North Pole, South Pole

Magnetic force is not equally strong in all parts of a magnet. Instead, there are two powerful points, called **poles**: the **north pole** and the **south pole**.

Once you know about poles, you know why magnets sometimes attract and sometimes repel each other. Poles that are *different* attract each other. The north pole of one magnet attracts the south pole of another and vice versa. Poles that are the *same* repel each other. One south pole repels another south pole, and a north pole repels a north pole.

Take Your Marbles for a Spin

Your bar magnet has markings on it that tell you which is the north (N) and which is the south (S) pole. Use your bar magnet to find the north and south poles of the marbles.

1. Place a marble on a table and slowly bring the south pole of the bar magnet close to it.
2. The marble should spin around until its north pole is sticking to the south pole of the bar magnet.
3. Now try this: Leave one marble on the table and hold the other marble in the air about 1 inch above it. Move the top marble in a slow circle around the marble on the table. The marble on the table will spin around in a circle to keep one pole toward the marble in the air.

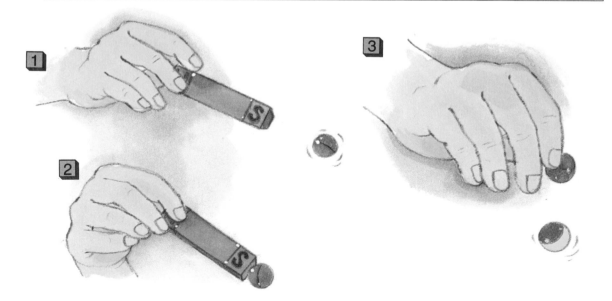

Magnetic or Not?

You know that magnets will attract or repel other magnets. But is that the only thing a magnet will affect? Will a magnet stick to you? Try it. You'll find that a magnet will attract some things, but not others.

Object	Magnet Sticks ?
refrigerator	yes
friend	no
aluminum can	
coins	
towel	
Nolan the cat	no
knife	
paper clip	yes
scissors	

Try It Yourself!

Magnetic Explorer

Search your home for things that are attracted by your bar magnet. Try sticking the magnet on as many objects as you can and write down the results.

Magnetic Metals

How many things did you find that your magnet would attract? You probably found that it would only attract certain kinds of metal. In fact, there are only a few kinds of metal a magnet will attract. **Iron** and **nickel** are the most common. Many things in your home are made of steel, which is made from iron.

But what about nickel? Will a 5¢ coin stick to your magnet? Try it and see. Unless your nickel comes from Canada, it won't. The American coin is now mostly copper.

Ghostly Powers

Magnetism can be very mysterious. It can go through things, as a ghost might pass through a solid wall.

What kinds of things will magnetism go through? Make a guess, then try this activity to see if you're right!

Material	What happens?
aluminum foil	nothing
cardboard	clip moves
leather	
steel cookie sheet	
plywood	
plastic	

Magnetic Magic Test

1. Gather different materials from your home. Each thing must be flat and thin: pieces of leather, cardboard, aluminum foil, plywood, plastic, and a steel cookie sheet, for example. You will also need a paper clip.
2. Place your bar magnet on one side and a paper clip on the other side of one material at a time.
3. Move the magnet to see if it will attract the paper clip through each kind of material. Record what happens.

Stronger Than Gravity

Magnetism is a very strong force. You can feel how strongly magnets pull each other when you bring them close together.

Believe it or not, magnetism is stronger than **gravity**—the invisible force that pulls things down toward the ground. When you throw a ball, it's gravity that makes it fall back to earth. If you drop an egg on the floor, you can blame the mess on gravity.

But as strong as gravity is, magnetism is stronger. And you can prove it with the experiment on the opposite page.

Try It Yourself!

The Amazing Jumping Marble

1 Place one magnetic marble on a table. Stand a wooden or plastic ruler on one end so that the ruler is straight up and down.

2 Pick up another marble and hold it directly over the first one, about 3 inches above the table, as measured on the ruler.

3 Slowly lower the top marble toward the marble on the table. Before the top marble gets all the way down, the bottom marble will suddenly forget about gravity and leap up into the air to cling to the top marble.

4 Check the ruler to see how high the top marble is when this happens.

Test a different top marble to see if it makes the bottom marble leap to the same point on the ruler. Does it leap higher than the first? Not as high as the first?

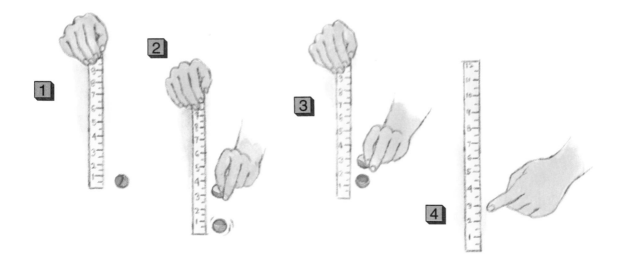

Magnetism Is Catching!

In a magnet or a magnetic metal, the atoms are arranged in microscopic sections called **domains**. Each domain is like a tiny magnet, with its own north and south poles.

In a magnet all of the domains are lined up with their north poles all pointing in the same direction. When the magnet comes near iron or nickel, its magnetism causes the domains in the metal to line up the same way. As the domains line up in the metal, it becomes a magnet and can even turn another piece of metal into a magnet!

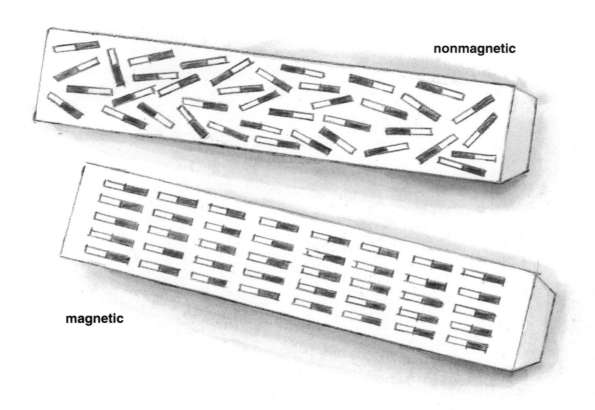

nonmagnetic

magnetic

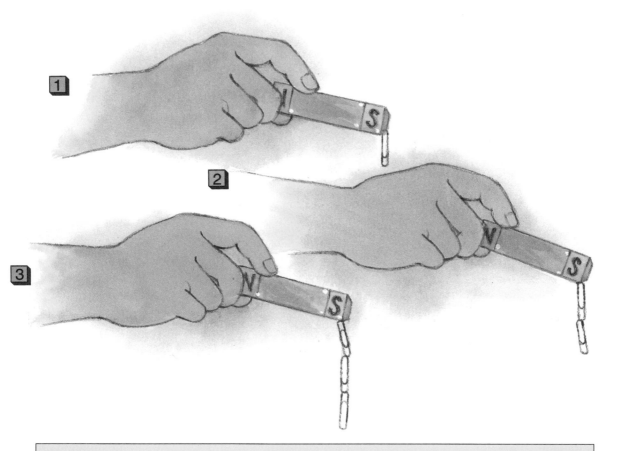

Try It Yourself!

Magic Paper Clip Chain

1 Hold a bar magnet in one hand and hang a paper clip on the magnet's end, so that most of the clip sticks out.

2 Attach a second paper clip to the first one, end-to-end.

3 Add a third paper clip. See how long you can make the chain. Now gently slide the first paper clip off the bar magnet. What happens to your chain?

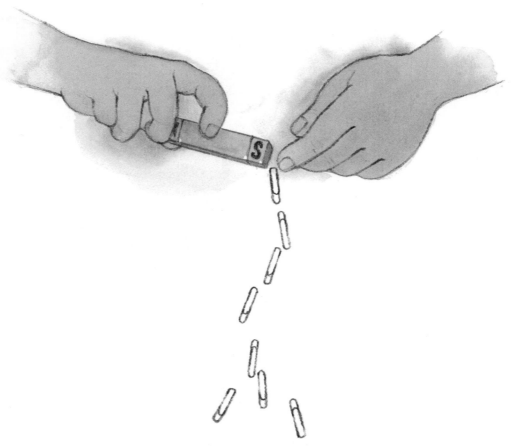

Making Magnets

The paper clips were magnets only as long as they were touching the bar magnet.

When you slid the first paper clip off the magnet, all the paper clips fell because they stopped being magnets the moment they left your bar magnet.

You can also turn iron or nickel into semi-permanent magnets. This activity shows you how—and how you can use your new magnet.

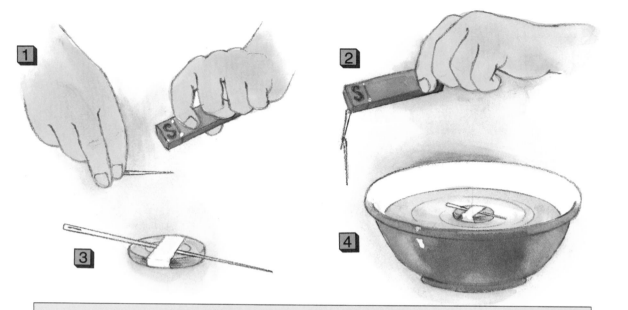

Try It Yourself!

Make a Compass

1. Hold a steel sewing needle by the dull end. Stroke the needle, from the dull end down to the point, with the south pole of a bar magnet. Stroke in only one direction. When you reach the point, move the magnet away from the needle before bringing it back to the dull end to start your next stroke.

2. Stroke the needle about sixty times, or until the needle is magnetized. It will have become a semi-permanent magnet.

3. Tape the needle to a medium-size button or cut out the circular bottom of a Styrofoam cup and tape the needle to it.

4. Float the needle in a bowl of water. The needle will turn slowly until it is pointing north.

Congratulations! You have made your own compass.

The Biggest Magnet of All

When you stroked your needle with the south pole of the bar magnet, you turned the sharp end of the needle into the south pole of a magnet. And what attracts the south pole of a magnet? The north pole of another magnet.

Your magnetic needle turns to point northward because the earth is a gigantic magnet. The earth's North and South Poles really are magnetic poles. We usually don't notice the earth's magnetism because it is very weak. But it is strong enough to make your compass turn in its bowl of water.

clock radio

computer

telephone

videotape

Magnetism Everywhere

Magnets and magnetism work for you every day. Telephones use magnets to turn sound into electricity. A videotape player uses magnets to play both sound and pictures. The videotape itself is made up of millions of magnetic particles glued to the tape.

The electricity that powers it all is made with the help of magnets. Without a magnetic compass, explorers like Columbus might never have found their way across the oceans. Without magnets, our world would be very different.